America's Game

Toronto
Blue Jays

Paul Joseph

ABDO & Daughters
PUBLISHING

Published by Abdo & Daughters, 4940 Viking Dr., Suite 622, Edina, MN 55435.

Cover photo: Allsport
Interior photos: Wide World Photo, pages 1, 4, 9, 10, 13-16, 21-23, 25, 27.

Edited by Kal Gronvall

Library of Congress Cataloging–in–Publication Data

Joseph, Paul, 1970-
    Toronto Blue Jays / Paul Joseph
        p. cm. — (America's game)
    Includes index.
    Summary: Details the history of the Toronto Blue Jays, an American League expansion franchise that won their division title within ten years and have won four more since then.
    ISBN   1-56239-679-X
    1. Toronto Blue Jays (Baseball team)—Juvenile literature.
[1. Toronto Blue Jays (Baseball team)—History. 2. Baseball—History.] I. Title. II. Series.
GV875.T67J67   1997
796.357' 64' 09713541—dc20   96-23780
                                                         CIP
                                                         AC

Contents

Toronto Blue Jays

Starting an expansion team is one of the hardest jobs in all of sports. Most expansion teams have to make do with players who have never been in the majors. Expansion teams also get old players who have been in the league many years, and are well past their prime.

In 1977, the American League (AL) added two teams, one of which was the Toronto Blue Jays. In the beginning, Toronto was like any other expansion franchise—they had players that most teams didn't want.

But the Blue Jays weren't discouraged. They had a plan, and they made it work. Within 10 years the Blue Jays would capture the division title. No other American League expansion franchise has risen as far and as fast as the Toronto Blue Jays.

Since 1987, the team has won four more division titles, two AL pennants, and two World Championships. They have assembled great teams with a mixture of solid defense, powerful hitting, and an all-around excellent pitching staff.

To house their up-and-coming team, the Toronto Blue Jays have built one of the most modern and beautiful stadiums in all of sports. They continue to fill the stadium with fans, and to put good teams on the field. The Blue Jays have gone from an expansion team to one of the most well-respected and envied franchises in Major League Baseball.

Joe Carter smashes a ninth-inning home run to win Game 6 of the 1993 World Series against Philadelphia.

A Long Wait For A Team

Many believed the city of Toronto would be an excellent place for a Major League Baseball team—even as far back as the 1800s. A.G. Spalding, one of the founders of the National League (NL), is said to have pushed for Toronto as a franchise in 1886. That never happened, but the city did get a minor league team. In 1895, the Toronto Maple Leafs were formed as part of the International League. The team featured many former and future major leaguers, and stayed in Toronto until 1967.

In 1976, Toronto nearly landed a major league franchise. The NL's San Francisco Giants were almost sold to a group of Toronto businessmen. But the deal fell through, and the Giants stayed put.

Later that year the American League voted to expand from 12 to 14 teams by adding franchises in Toronto and Seattle. Finally, after nearly 100 years of waiting, the city of Toronto had its major league franchise. It wasn't a National League team, and it wasn't an already established franchise, but it was theirs. And for $7 million, it was only about half the price it would have cost to buy the Giants.

The city of Toronto was very excited to see its new team play. First on the agenda was picking a team name. In a "Name That Team" contest 30,000 people sent their suggestions. The team went with the name that was chosen the most—Blue Jays.

Next the team needed to acquire front office people, coaches, and players. In less than one year the Blue Jays had to play a regular season game—and it wouldn't be an easy task.

A Cold Beginning

The Toronto Blue Jays' organization hired Pat Gillick as vice president for player personnel. Gillick had previously worked for the New York Yankees. He had the toughest job in baseball—fielding an expansion team. But he had a well thought-out plan to build the young team. It included finding solid leadership, well-respected veteran players, and an excellent minor league system. But most of all he needed time.

Gillick hired Roy Hartsfield to be the Toronto Blue Jays manager. Hartsfield had total control on the field, and was well-liked by his team. He knew the game well from his experience as a former second basemen in the majors for the Boston Braves.

Before the Blue Jays could take the field, though, they had to fix the stadium in which they would be playing. Exhibition Stadium was built in 1957—for football. A baseball game had never been played there. Major construction was needed to turn it into a baseball stadium.

Many seats were installed, and an outfield fence was built. Beyond the outfield fence was a large section of grass, which was actually the rest of the football field. It wasn't the prettiest stadium for baseball, but it would have to make do until the Blue Jays built their own stadium.

Nonetheless, Exhibition Stadium was ready when opening day came. On April 7, 1977, the Toronto Blue Jays played their first game. Although it was the beginning of the baseball season, it was more like hockey weather. More than 44,000 fans showed up in frigid 30-degree temperatures to see their new team play its first game.

The Blue Jays hosted the Chicago White Sox, who took an early 2-0 lead. When it was the Blue Jays' turn to bat, rookie first baseman Doug Ault slammed a pitch over the wall in left center field. The cold Toronto fans, in snow suits and boots, went wild.

Then in the third inning Ault went deep again for home run number two! There was now utter pandemonium at Exhibition Stadium. The fans were acting as if the Blue Jays had just won the World Series.

The Blue Jays went on to win their first-ever game 9-5. Although Doug Ault didn't go on to do much in the major leagues, he will always be remembered by Toronto baseball fans for his two homers in that first game.

After that first win the Blue Jays didn't capture many more. They finished the year losing 107 games. But there were some highlights. Bob Bailor hit .310, and pitcher Dave Lemanczyk won 13 games. But the best news of all was that nearly two million faithful fans showed up to watch the Blue Jays in their inaugural season.

There was little improvement for the Blue Jays in their second year, in which they lost 102 games. In 1979 it got even worse. They lost 109 games and finished the season more than 50 games out of first place.

Although it looked bad for the hapless Toronto Blue Jays, they were still following their original plan for building the team. And believe it or not, there was some hope. Home run hitter John Mayberry came over from the Kansas City Royals and crushed more than 20 homers in 1978 and 1979. Rookie defensive whiz Alfredo Griffin played a mean shortstop, and batted .287 on his way to Rookie of the Year in 1979.

Also in 1979, the Blue Jays got to see how their plan was unfolding in the minors. Pitcher Dave Stieb moved up through the minors and started for the Blue Jays in 1979. He picked up eight wins that year—but that was only the start.

The Blue Jays' John Mayberry follows through on a fourth-inning home run during a game against the New York Mets.

Dave Stieb sends a ball to the plate during a 1990 game against the Cleveland Indians in which Stieb threw a no-hitter.

Signs Of Improvement

In 1980, Bobby Mattick took over as manager for the Blue Jays. Finally the team finished the year losing fewer than 100 games. They did, however, finish in last place.

But there were signs of life. Two young pitchers began to blossom. Jim Clancy won 13 games and an improved Dave Stieb won 12 in his first full season with the Blue Jays.

John Mayberry led the team in home runs again, crushing 30. But the best news was their farm system. Outfielder Lloyd Moseby and first baseman Willie Upshaw moved up through the ranks of the minors to become future stars.

In 1981, there was a lengthy players' strike that left Major League Baseball in disarray with a shorter split season. That year there was little team improvement, but the building continued.

Dave Stieb continued to shine, winning 11 games (because of the strike, the most wins recorded that year was 14). And two new faces showed up from the Blue Jays' budding farm system, George Bell and Jesse Barfield, who would also go on to be future stars for the team.

At the end of the season, manager Bobby Mattick was fired and replaced by Bobby Cox. And Danny Ainge, who was supposed to star for the Blue Jays, quit after three years to try his luck at basketball. Basketball worked much better for Ainge, who did indeed star in the NBA for the Boston Celtics.

Continuing With The Plan

Bobby Cox took over the reigns as skipper of the Blue Jays in 1982. Fans and management were counting on Cox to finally move the team out of the cellar.

Toronto was still focused on their plan. They were beginning to see signs of greatness in their farm system, and of course, they still needed time to build a winner.

Pitcher Dave Stieb was getting better each year, winning 17 games in 1982. Jim Clancy and Luis Leal were also showing signs of improvement on the hill, picking up 16 and 12 wins respectively.

Willie Upshaw replaced John Mayberry at first base and led the team with homers (21) and RBIs (75). A young, talented outfield in George Bell, Lloyd Moseby, and Jesse Barfield had All-Star written all over them.

Alfredo Griffin was still the man at short, and second baseman Damasco Garcia led the Blue Jays with a .310 batting average.

This young team finally moved out of the cellar and tied for sixth place in the AL East. It wasn't great, but the Blue Jays' organization could finally see the light at the end of the tunnel. Pat Gillick stuck with his plan, and it was about to pay off.

Willie Upshaw follows through on a fly ball to right field during a game against the Baltimore Orioles.

Doyle Alexander fires a pitch against the New York Yankees.

AL East Champions

In 1983, the Blue Jays had their first winning season, finishing only nine games behind the division champion Baltimore Orioles. Dave Stieb continued to excel, winning 17 games and striking out 187. The Blue Jays also added Doyle Alexander, a solid pitcher from the Yankees, to help the staff.

Moseby, Garcia, and Upshaw each batted over .300. The team home run total climbed to 167, with Upshaw (27), Barfield (27), and new designated hitter Cliff Johnson (22) leading the way.

In 1984, Toronto kept up their assault with awesome pitching and powerful hitting. They won 89 games on their way to a second-place finish.

Dave Stieb picked up 16 wins but was outdone by teammate Doyle Alexander, who had 17 wins—the most in the league. George Bell had nearly a .300 batting average while crushing 26 dingers, 39 doubles, and 87 RBIs.

For the Toronto Blue Jays, 1984 was the best season ever up to this point. Toronto kept pursuing their long-term plan to build a winner. And their patience paid off even further the next year.

Filled with confidence, Toronto took their solid line-up into the 1985 season. They played well all year long, and in a down-to-the-wire race, grabbed their first-ever American League East Pennant.

The team featured one of the best outfields in Barfield, Moseby, and Bell, who combined for 73 homers and 250 RBIs.

The pitching was again key. Left-hander Jimmy Key, who was in his second year, picked up 14 wins. Stieb also added 14 wins and had the league's lowest earned run average (ERA) with 2.48. Doyle Alexander had another solid year, leading the team in wins with 17.

After the best regular season in franchise history, the Blue Jays couldn't move on. They played their hearts out in the American League Championship Series (ALCS) against the AL West Champion Kansas City Royals. The series went the distance, with the Royals winning in a nailbiting seventh game on their way to grabbing the American League pennant.

Although the Blue Jays lost the ALCS, they were not discouraged. They figured that with a young and talented team they would be back the next year. But it was not to be.

Blue Jays' pitcher Jimmy Key in action during the 1985 All-Star Game in Minneapolis, Minnesota.

Disappointing Finishes

After winning the AL East title in 1985, Bobby Cox took off for the Atlanta Braves, and Jimy Williams took over as manager. Williams couldn't get the team to repeat in 1986, as Toronto finished in fourth place. Pitching was something the Blue Jays could always count on, but not this year. Stieb, Key, and Alexander all had disappointing seasons.

But the hitting was still there. Tony Fernandez led the team with a .310 batting average. Jesse Barfield led the league in homers with 40, and also added 108 RBIs. George Bell hit a whopping .309 and kept pace with Barfield with 108 RBIs.

In 1987, it looked as though the Blue Jays would bounce back. The team had the AL East crown all but wrapped up. The only thing they needed was one win in their three-game series against the Detroit Tigers near the end of the season. But the Tigers swept the series and took the AL East crown with them.

George Bell had an awesome season, grabbing the league's Most Valuable Player (MVP) Award. Bell batted .308, smashed 47 homers, and added 134 RBIs.

In 1988, the team came up short again, finishing a disappointing third place. The most talented team in baseball could not seem to win the division. In 1989 things would change. A new manager would take over, the Blue Jays would begin play in their new stadium, and they would grab their second AL East pennant.

Facing page: George Bell hits against the Baltimore Orioles.

Toronto

In 1980, John Mayberry led the Blue Jays in home runs, crushing 30.

In 1985, Dave Stieb had the league's lowest ERA with 2.48.

Willie Upshaw batted over .300 in 1983, smacking 27 home runs.

George Bell won the AL MVP Award in 1987.

Blue Jays

Fred McGriff hit the first home run in the Toronto SkyDome in June 1989.

In 1990, at the age of 40, Dave Winfield batted .290 and hit 26 home runs.

Roberto Alomar led the Blue Jays in 1992 with a .310 batting average and 177 hits.

Joe Carter is only one of two players to ever end a World Series with a home run, when he did it in 1992.

Cito And The SkyDome

The much-talented Toronto Blue Jays started off the 1989 season horribly. Their first problem was that their new stadium was behind schedule. Secondly, after 36 games the Blue Jays had managed only 12 victories. To try to solve that losing problem, Williams was fired, and Cito Gaston took over as new skipper.

Gaston, Toronto's former batting coach, was supposed to be an interim manager until they could find a permanent replacement. But while they were looking, Gaston led the Blue Jays to victory after victory.

Finally in June of 1989, after waiting more than 12 years, the Toronto Blue Jays got a new home. Their new stadium, called the SkyDome, was something to see. And many people came out to see it. The 1991 season saw over four million fans go through the gate—no other major league team has ever come near that yearly attendance figure.

The futuristic SkyDome has a retractable roof that can be opened or closed in less than 30 minutes. The SkyDome is perfect for a city that can be very cold and even has snow in the early and late parts of the season. At the north end of the stadium is a 364-room hotel, with 70 of those rooms overlooking the playing field!

The awesome stadium hosted the Milwaukee Brewers in the first game ever played in the SkyDome. Fred McGriff pounded the first home run in the new stadium, much to the delight of the Toronto fans. But it wouldn't be enough, as the Brewers grabbed the first-ever victory in the SkyDome.

Although they lost that first game in the SkyDome, they didn't lose many more that year. The Blue Jays fought it out down-to-the-wire and won the AL East pennant on the last weekend of the season.

George Bell led the team offensively in 1989, with a .297 batting average and 104 RBIs. He was helped out by Fred McGriff, who smashed 36 homers and 92 RBIs. Dave Stieb again led the team on the hill with 17 wins.

The talented Blue Jays didn't have enough to get past the AL West Champion Oakland Athletics. The A's were led by Jose Canseco, Rickey Henderson, Dave Stewart, and Dennis Eckersley, who easily manhandled the Blue Jays, four games to one.

In 1989, the Blue Jays came back and had another excellent year. But it wasn't enough. They finished the season in second place, only two games out of first. Dave Stieb continued to star on the mound, grabbing 18 wins. New players John Olerud and Pat Borders showed that they could play in the majors. And nearly four million fans jammed the SkyDome. Overall it was a very successful year, but the Blue Jays and their fans wanted more.

First baseman Fred McGriff backhands a ground ball during a game against the California Angels.

Dave Winfield batting during Game 6 of the 1992 World Series against the Atlanta Braves.

World Champions

In 1991, the Toronto Blue Jays lost some great players but gained even better ones. Slugger Joe Carter, outfielder Devon White, second baseman Roberto Alomar, and pitcher Juan Guzman were all new faces who helped lead the multi-talented Blue Jays to their third AL East title.

In the ALCS the Blue Jays were matched up against the underdog Minnesota Twins. The Twins were led by Kirby Puckett, Kent Hrbek, Greg Gagne, and Jack Morris. Minnesota played with more heart and seemed to want the series more than the Blue Jays did. The Twins easily dismantled Toronto in five games, and went on to win the 1991 World Series.

The Toronto Blue Jays' organization and fans couldn't figure out the problem, but they never gave up. The Blue Jays came back in 1992 and had a historic year. The Jays easily captured their fourth AL East crown. They added 40-year-old Dave Winfield, who proved he still had a lot of baseball in him. He batted .290, cracked 26 home runs, and belted 108 RBIs. Joe Carter also was on fire, smashing 34 dingers, and had a whopping 119 RBIs. Roberto Alomar led all Blue Jay hitters, though, with a .310 batting average, and 177 hits.

On the hill, free-agent acquisition Jack Morris, who the year before led the Twins to a World Championship, led the Jays with 21 wins. Juan Guzman added 16, and Jimmy Key 13.

Roberto Alomar watches his two-run homer head for the right field wall during a 1992 ALCS game against the Oakland A's.

This time the Blue Jays would not be denied. They outlasted the always-tough Oakland A's in the ALCS, taking the series four games to two. The Blue Jays, after previously being denied three times, were on their way to their first-ever World Series.

In the 1992 Series Toronto was matched against the National League Champion Atlanta Braves. Everyone knew the Series was going to have some fine pitching. The Braves were returning with the same awesome pitching staff that led them to the World Series the previous year. Tom Glavine, John Smoltz, Steve Avery, and Charlie Leibrandt were on the hill, with Terry Pendleton, Ron Gant, Dave Justice, and Sid Bream picking up the offensive duties for the Braves.

But the Blue Jays had a lineup that was just as solid. Baseball fans throughout North America were excited for this match-up. Game 1 was a pitchers' duel, with the Braves' Tom Glavine outdueling the Jays' Jack Morris, 3-1.

Game 2 featured a come-from-behind, ninth inning, 5-4 victory for the Blue Jays, who tied the Series, 1-1. The third game of the Series was also decided in the ninth inning, again in Toronto's favor. Jimmy Key picked up a close 2-1, Game 4 victory, giving the Blue Jays a commanding 3-1 Series lead.

The Braves didn't give up, as they captured Game 5 behind the pitching of John Smoltz. The Braves continued to play tough the following game. Behind 3-2 in the Series, they took Game 6 to extra innings, as they tied it up the ninth inning.

In the top of the 11th inning, Dave Winfield doubled to score two runs, and the Jays had a 4-2 lead. But the Braves came back and scored one—but that would be it. The Blue Jays won 4-3 and captured the World Championship—the first-ever for the Blue Jays, and the first-ever for a team that resides outside the United States.

It was a historic day for baseball and for baseball fans in Canada. But the Jays weren't satisfied with just one World Championship. They came back the next year and won it in an unbelievable way.

Joe Carter celebrates his World Series home run in 1993.

Oh Joe, What A Finish!

The Toronto Blue Jays wanted to come back and win another title. In the off-season they got rid of many players and added a dozen new ones, including Paul Molitor and Dave Stewart. For the stretch-drive they picked up speedster Rickey Henderson, who added enough fire to get them another AL East crown.

First baseman John Olerud not only led the Blue Jays in hitting, he led the entire league—but he had to get by teammates Paul Molitor and Roberto Alomar, who finished right behind him.

After flirting with .400 through August, Olerud ended the year with a .363 average. Paul Molitor led the league in hits with 211, while Duane Ward led the league from the hill with 45 saves.

After winning 95 regular season games, the Blue Jays captured their third consecutive AL East pennant. It took the Blue Jays six games to get by the AL West Champion Chicago White Sox, and then they headed to their second consecutive World Series.

The Blue Jays were matched against the Philadelphia Phillies in the Fall Classic. The teams split the first two games in Toronto. The Blue Jays grabbed the third game, for a 2-1 Series lead.

The fourth game was a record breaker. Both teams were scoring run after run. By the eighth inning the Phillies had a commanding 14-9 lead. But the Jays came back to score six runs in the top of the eighth to take the lead. The Blue Jays held on and won the highest-scoring World Series game in history, by a score of 15-14.

The Toronto Blue Jays needed only one more win to become back-to-back World Champions. But Philadelphia wasn't going to hand it to them. The Phillies grabbed the fifth game, 2-0.

In Game 6 it looked as though the Phillies were going to tie the Series at three games each. They came back from a 5-1 deficit to take the lead 6-5 in the top of the ninth. All Philadelphia needed was three outs and they would force a seventh game.

The Phillies got their first two outs. Then Joe Carter stepped up to the plate for the Blue Jays, with two men on. On a 2-2 pitch, Carter extended his long arms over the plate and smashed the ball toward left field. It was over—the ball cleared the wall and the Toronto Blue Jays were World Champions again.

Joe Carter is only one of two players to ever end a World Series with a home run. Carter's homer touched off a thunderous roar. The celebration continued on the streets of Toronto until the next day.

Facing page: Members of the Toronto Blue Jays mob teammate Joe Carter after his Series-winning home run in Game 6 against the Philadelphia Phillies.

Stalled

After winning back-to-back World Series Championships, the Toronto Blue Jays came out in 1994 to try to make it three. But it was all for naught, as the season was canceled due to the players' strike.

In 1995, the Blue Jays went from consecutive World Championships to the cellar, grabbing last place in the AL East, and earning a tie for the worst record in all of baseball.

Right now the future doesn't look very bright for this once-solid franchise. The team does, however, still pack the fans into the SkyDome, and the front office is continuing to build.

It seems safe to say that the Toronto Blue Jays' organization, which started with a great plan and captured a pennant in less than 10 years, and later added 2 World Championships, has another plan to get the team going again.

The most successful American League expansion franchise will soon fly high again.

Glossary

All-Star: A player who is voted by fans as the best player at one position in a given year.

American League (AL): An association of baseball teams formed in 1900 which make up one-half of the major leagues.

American League Championship Series (ALCS): A best-of-seven-game playoff with the winner going to the World Series to face the National League Champions.

Batting Average: A baseball statistic calculated by dividing a batter's hits by the number of times at bat.

Earned Run Average (ERA): A baseball statistic which calculates the average number of runs a pitcher gives up per nine innings of work.

Fielding Average: A baseball statistic which calculates a fielder's success rate based on the number of chances the player has to record an out.

Hall of Fame: A memorial for the greatest baseball players of all time, located in Cooperstown, New York.

Home Run (HR): A play in baseball where a batter hits the ball over the outfield fence scoring everyone on base as well as the batter.

Major Leagues: The highest ranking associations of professional baseball teams in the world, currently consisting of the American and National Baseball Leagues.

Minor Leagues: A system of professional baseball leagues at levels below Major League Baseball.

National League (NL): An association of baseball teams formed in 1876 which make up one-half of the major leagues.

National League Championship Series (NLCS): A best-of-seven-game playoff with the winner going to the World Series to face the American League Champions.

Pennant: A flag which symbolizes the championship of a professional baseball league.

Pitcher: The player on a baseball team who throws the ball for the batter to hit. The pitcher stands on a mound and pitches the ball toward the strike zone area above the plate.

Plate: The place on a baseball field where a player stands to bat. It is used to determine the width of the strike zone. Forming the point of the diamond-shaped field, it is the final goal a base runner must reach to score a run.

RBI: A baseball statistic standing for *runs batted in.* Players receive an RBI for each run that scores on their hits.

Rookie: A first-year player, especially in a professional sport.

Slugging Percentage: A statistic which points out a player's ability to hit for extra bases by taking the number of total bases hit and dividing it by the number of at bats.

Stolen Base: A play in baseball when a base runner advances to the next base while the pitcher is delivering the pitch.

Strikeout: A play in baseball when a batter is called out for failing to put the ball in play after the pitcher has delivered three strikes.

Triple Crown: A rare accomplishment when a single player finishes a season leading their league in batting average, home runs, and RBIs. A pitcher can win a Triple Crown by leading the league in wins, ERA, and strikeouts.

Walk: A play in baseball when a batter receives four pitches out of the strike zone and is allowed to go to first base.

World Series: The championship of Major League Baseball played since 1903 between the pennant winners from the American and National Leagues.

Index